The Trailer Park Princesses

Story by Pete Marlowe
Art by Leanne Franson

ANNICK PRESS

TORONTO + NEW YORK + VANCOUVER

Annick Press Ltd.

We acknowledge the support of the Canada Council for the Arts, the Ontario
Arts Council, and the Government of Canada through the Book Publishing
Industry Development Program (BPIDP) for our publishing activities.

Cataloguing in Publication Data

Marlowe, Pete
The trailer park princesses

ISBN 1-55037-617-9 (bound)   ISBN 1-55037-616-0 (pbk.)

I. Franson, Leanne. II. Title.

PS8576.A74175T72 2000   jC813'.54   C99-932641-4
PZ7.M37Tr 2000

Distributed in Canada by:

Firefly Books Ltd.
3680 Victoria Park Avenue
Willowdale, Ontario
M2H 3K1

Published in the U.S.A. by:

Annick Press (U.S.) Ltd.

Distributed in the U.S.A. by:

Firefly Books (U.S.) Inc.
P.O. Box 1338
Ellicot Station
Buffalo, New York   14205

Printed and bound in Canada
by Friesens, Altona, Manitoba.

The art in this book was rendered in acrylic with pencil.
The text was typeset in New Baskerville and Remedy.

for Veronica,
being seven
P.M.

For my mom, Elaine
L.F.

"How did it go again?" asked Rebecca.

"Once upon a time," said Jane.

"Oh, yes," said Rebecca.

"In a land far, far away."

"Yes, I remember that part."

"There were four princesses.
And the four princesses all looked exactly the same."

"Just like us," said Rebecca.

"Yes," said Jane. "Just like us."

"Did they have a very wonderful life?"

"Yes. They had a very wonderful life.
  They lived in a beautiful palace.
  Their mother was the queen of all the land."

"Did they have horses?"

"They had horses and birthday parties and beds that
  had curtains, and the other children all loved them."

"Was there an earthquake?"

"Not yet. It seemed like their very wonderful life
  would go on forever."

"And then what happened?"
"There was an earthquake."
"Without any warning?"
"Without any warning. There had never been
such an earthquake in that faraway land.
The four princesses woke up in their canopied
beds, and their mother rushed in."

"Were they very brave?"
"They were very brave. And the royal bedchamber rocked
and swayed, and the walls were like the waves of the sea."
"And did the floor disappear?"

"One half of the room fell away, and two princesses were
tumbled out of their bed curtains, and down.
And down went their mother as well."

"And the other two sisters?"

"They jumped out of their beds, and they looked down the hole.
And the earthquake was such a big earthquake that the ground shook,
and time shook as well.

And the two princesses
and their mother fell
into **Ancient Egypt,**

and the earth **shook** again.

And they fell
into the **Wild West**,

and the earth **shook** once more.

And they fell into the backyard
of the Trailer Park,

and the earth stood still."

"What happened to their mother?"
"She bumped her head when she landed,
and she didn't remember a thing."
"Not a thing?"
"Not one single thing. And they all lived in the Trailer Park
forever after, but the two princesses never forgot."
"No," said Rebecca. "They never forgot."

"Lights out now," said their mother. And their lights went out now, and they lay in the darkness.

"And do you remember," said Jane, "what happened to the other two sisters?"
"Yes," said Rebecca. "When the palace stopped quaking, they went to
the royal countinghouse, and they told the king what had happened.
And the king fell into a deep sadness."

"Yes," said Jane. "He did."

"And he called to his royal coachman, and summoned his royal coach, and sent to the royal stables for a royal team of horses. And the two other princesses mounted the coach and set out to search for their sisters."

"And for the queen?"
"And for the queen as well. They rumbled as fast as they
could down cobblestone streets, till the royal coach rattled
and jostled, then faster, till time rattled and jostled as well.

They found clues
in **Ancient Egypt,**

and they found clues
in the **Wild West**.

And every day they're coming closer and closer to the end of their search.
One day they will turn off the highway, come past the arena, enter the Trailer Park,
and drive up the hill. It might be tomorrow."
"Yes," said Jane. "It might be."

"Good night, Princess Jane."
"Good night, Princess Rebecca."
They slept, and dreamed.
And their mother said:

"Time for breakfast."

They rushed to the front window in their pajamas,

and they looked out, down the hill, to the edge of the Trailer Park,

past the arena, and out to the highway.

"What do you see?" asked their mother.

"The weather," said Rebecca.

"And leaves blowing from the trees," said Jane.

"And cars going off to work," said Rebecca.

"And nothing else," said Jane.

They sat down to breakfast.

"Brush your teeth," said their mother.
They brushed their teeth.

"And get dressed." They got dressed.

"And stop all that squabbling."
They stopped all that squabbling.
"You're going to be late.
Here's your lunches. Give me a kiss."

They walked backwards down the hill.
"Can you still see our trailer?"
"If I jump up maybe."
And then it was gone. They found a wind-fallen branch
and threw it off one side of the bridge into the creek.
They ran to the other side. They stopped at the pond to
see the baby muskrat.

"Good morning, princesses."

They turned that way, then this way,
and this way an old woman was feeding the ducks.

"Good morning," said Jane.
"How did you know?" said Rebecca.
"There are some things," said the old woman,
"you can just tell."
"She can just tell," said Rebecca.

Jane and Rebecca had never told anyone.
They looked at each other,
and made their thinking faces.

"Although it did make me wonder,"
the old woman said, "how two princesses
came to be living here in the Trailer Park.
Let me guess."

There must have been an earthquake.

And if there was an earthquake,
I bet time shook.

And if time shook,
your mother probably bumped her head.

Here, have some bread to feed the ducks."
"But what can we do about it all?" said Rebecca.
And the old woman said: "You can treat
your mother like a queen.
She is a queen, isn't she?"
Jane and Rebecca ripped up little
pieces of bread.
The ducks wobbled after them.
"You must feel very alone in this
new world," said the old woman.
"Except," said Rebecca.
"For each other," said Jane.
"Then perhaps no one has told
you," the old woman said,
"that there are a great
number of princesses here."

"Are there?" said Jane.

"Really?" said Rebecca.

"There have been many earthquakes,"
 said the old woman.

"That's true," said Rebecca.

"They happen all the time," said Jane.

"But," said the old woman, "when the princesses land,
 many of them bump their heads."

"So they don't remember?"

"Many of them don't. And the rest of them keep it a secret,
 just like you do. Because you can't very well go around
 acting like a princess in the Trailer Park."

"No, that's true," said Jane.

"The others might not understand," said Rebecca.

"So you never can tell," said the old woman, "who might be a princess,
but a secret one. You might even have a few in your class. And do you know,
I've heard a rumor lately that there's even a prince or two hiding somewhere
in the area."

"In this area?" said Rebecca.

"Hiding," said Jane.

"You better run," the old woman said.
"I think that's your school bus pulling in."
They ran up the hill.

They got the last seat together,
and they whispered.

"When you think about it," said Rebecca.
"Anyone we meet," said Jane.
"Yes," said Rebecca. "You never can tell."

They sat by the playground for recess.

They sat by the soccer field for lunch.

"Priscilla," said Rebecca.

"Maybe Sarah," said Jane.

"I bet Richard's one of the princes."

All the day long their eyes shone surprises to each other. And at the end of the day, the royal school bus dropped them off at the edge of the Trailer Park.

They stopped at the royal pond to greet the royal baby muskrat, threw royal branches from the royal bridge down into the royal creek, and walked up the royal hill.

"Can you see our trailer yet?"
"If I jump up maybe."
"Did you see it?"

"I saw a big wheel.

A big wheel with spokes."
"Yes. And I see two of them now.
And four of them."
"And horses."

They ran. At the top of the hill now, their mother was coming to meet them, running, in her old coat and old sandals. And she was wearing the crown.